MW01114883

My Name is Norman

written and photographed
by
Mia Coulton

My nose is black.

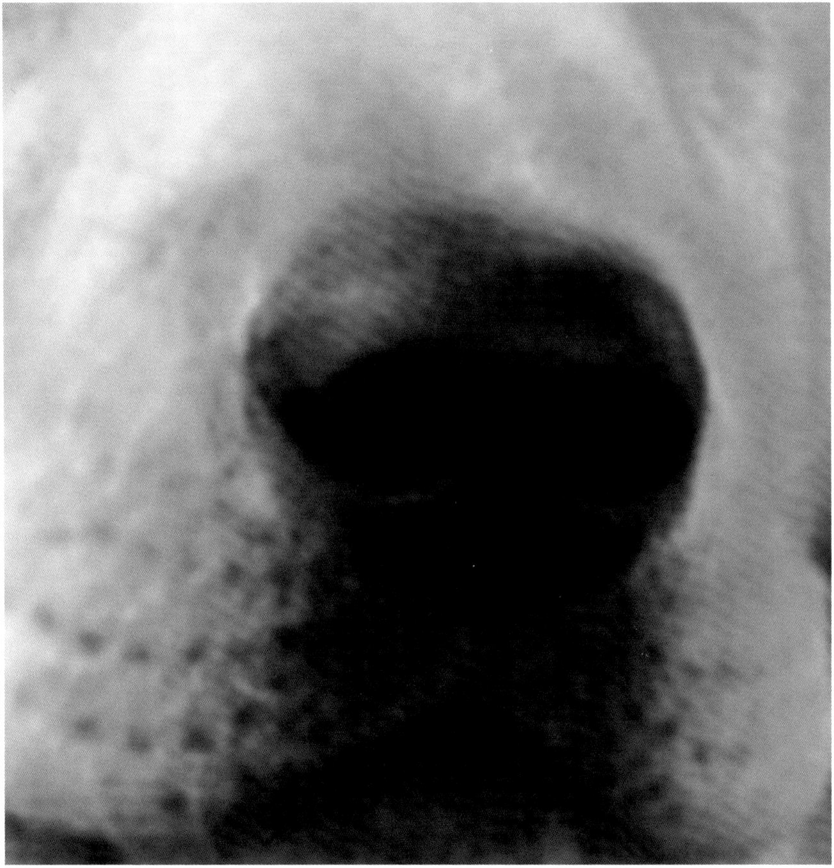

My eyes are brown.

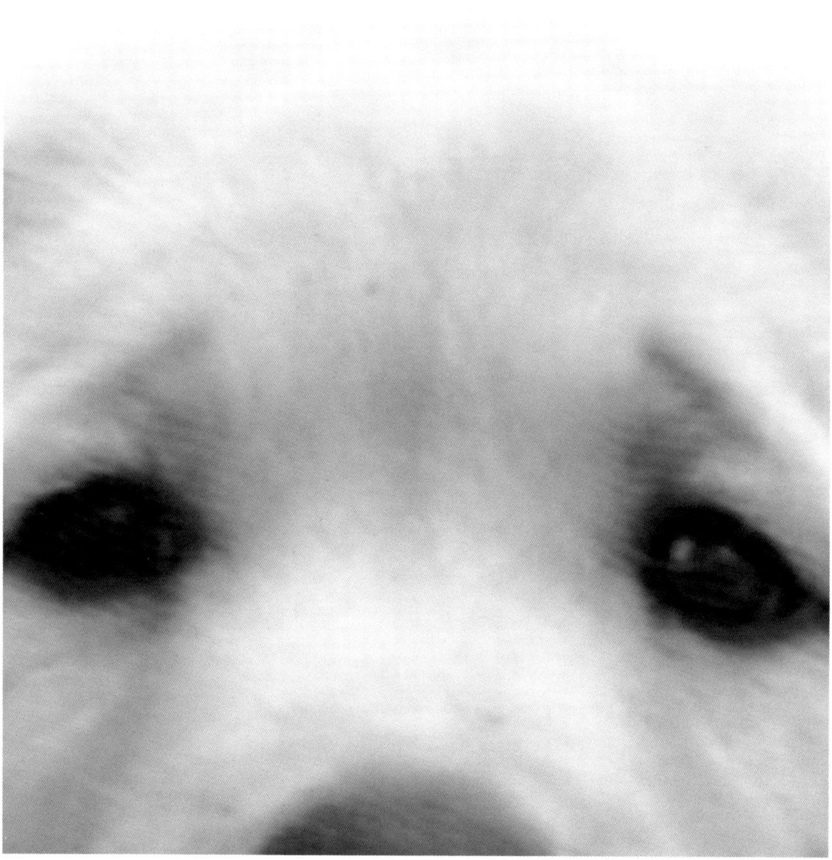

My tongue is pink.

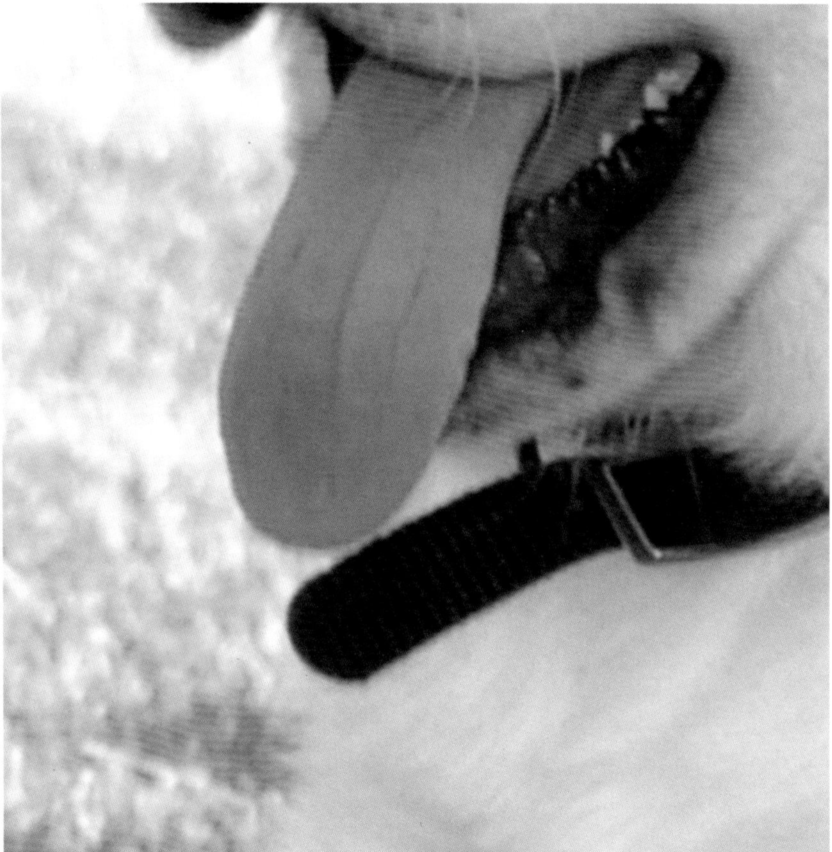

My fur is white.

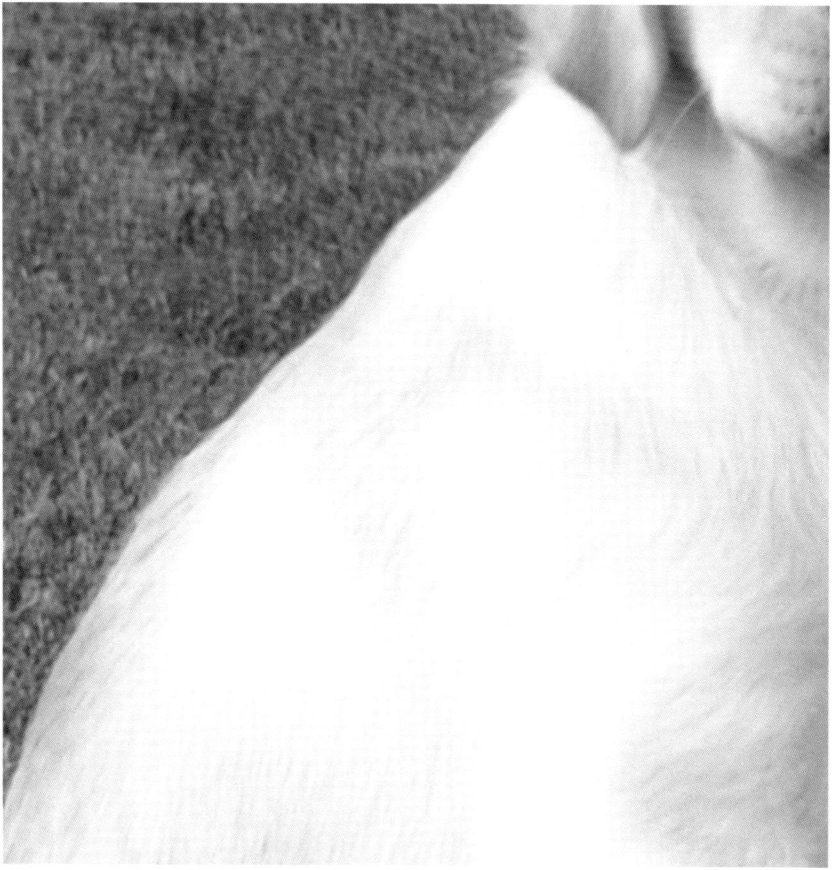

My collar is blue.

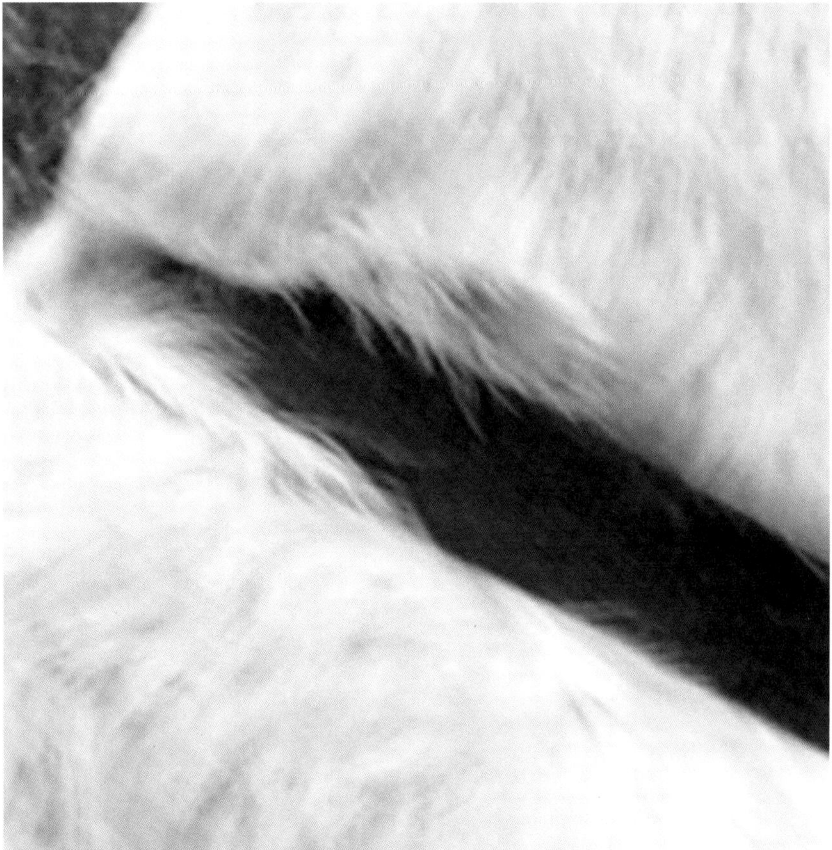

My name is Norman.

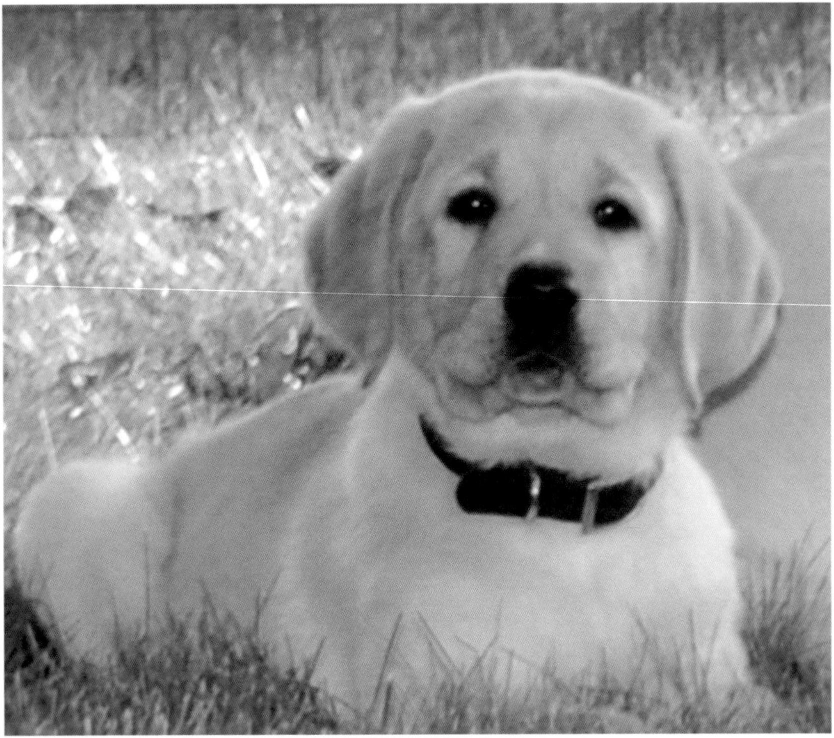